# SMELLY BILL
# LOVE STINKS

Daniel
Postgate

meadowside
CHILDREN'S

When Bill saw Peachy Snugglekins
Come trotting past the rubbish bins
His knees went weak, his eyes grew wide,
He felt all gooey deep inside.

He dropped his bag
of rotting stuff,
He'd seen enough,

He was in love.

He found a rose and snatched it up
Then ran to catch the lucky pup.
But when he saw who clutched her lead
His world turned very dim indeed...

The face of great Aunt Bleach stared down,
With curling lip and hateful frown.

'Get lost!'
she hollered.
'Go on,
shoo!

My Peach is far
too good for you!'

They marched straight past,
snouts in the air,
As if Bill simply wasn't there.

That night Bill couldn't sleep, instead
He climbed onto the garden shed

OOOO

OOOAAAAWWWOOOO

And howled and yowled up at the moon,
A loud and melancholy tune,
About the love he couldn't win
Because Peach was too good for him.

Next day, Bill's folks woke up to see
Something quite extraordinary:
Their stinking pet, sat in the tub...

# Begging for a soapy scrub!

Now later in the park that day
A 'dog parade' got underway.
The poshest dogs you'll ever see,
The finest in their pedigree,
Had come in every shape and size,
To try and win the
**'Best Dog'** prize.

Peach was also at the show
Splendid in her scarlet bow,
But who was that among the crowd,
Looking like an orange cloud
With crooked snout and snaggled teeth;
And very skinny legs
        beneath?

# What creature was it, can you tell?

# Why, it was Bill without the smell!
He'd come to prove he was as fine
As any fancy-pants canine.

The chatting crowd began to hush.
'He's like a walking
   toilet brush!'
Some rather nasty person sneered.

And while the others laughed and jeered,
Bill turned around and, in dismay,
He slowly, sadly, slunk away.

Just then the show was interrupted
When Vesuvius erupted.

**Vesuvius**, a giant hound,
Chased all the other
dogs around!

Then roaring, growling,
barking, snarling
Went for Great Aunt Bleach's darling!

Poor Peach shot off across the park.
She dashed into a forest, dark;
Hoping that he wouldn't find her,
**But the beast was right behind her!**

Straight in a boggy swamp she flew
And promptly sank into
the goo.

'Please save my
Peachy-kins!' Bleach cried
When all the other
folk arrived.

But they just snorted,
'No chance ducky,
We don't want our clothing mucky.'
Bleach howled and screamed,
she begged and wept...

Then suddenly a creature leapt
Straight in that dark and dirty bog
To save Aunt Bleach's precious dog.

Which
creature
was it,
can you tell?

Of course,
it was our
Smelly Bill!

Bleach hugged Bill to her grateful chest.
'I think we know which dog's the best...
Bill stinks, but he is brave and bold
And has a heart of solid gold!'

Then Bleach said
something very strange:

She whispered,
'Bill, please
never change.'

Later, when the day was done,
Our hero watched the evening sun
Turn slowly to a shade of red
And sink behind the garden shed.

He sat with his new sweetheart Peach,
Who he'd so bravely saved …

And next to them
sat Great Aunt Bleach

To make
sure they
behaved!

To all at
Whitstable Endowed
Junior School

First published in 2009
by Meadowside Children's Books
185 Fleet Street London EC4A 2HS
www.meadowsidebooks.com

A CIP catalogue record for this book
is available from the British Library
10 9 8 7 6 5 4 3 2 1
Printed in Indonesia